The Market Wedding

A Note from The PJ Library

Marriage

Jewish tradition teaches that from the time of the first couple, Adam and Eve, God recognized that it was preferable for humans to have partners. In addition to the companionship and support basic to having a mate, this also ensures the perpetuation of the Jewish people.

The Jewish Wedding

A traditional Jewish wedding takes place under a canopy called a chuppah. The canopy itself can be a prayer shawl or an artistically crafted piece, sometimes given to the couple by a loved one. The chuppah symbolizes the home and life that the new couple will build together; it is open on all sides to symbolize the welcome that guests will always receive from this couple.

Under the chuppah during the ceremony it is customary for the bride to circle the groom multiple times. In many contemporary Jewish weddings, three circles are made by each partner, representing the three repetitions of the phrase "I will betroth you to me," found in Hosea 2:21-22.

One of the most widely known customs of a Jewish wedding involves the breaking underfoot of a glass, accompanied by wishes of "Mazel Tov!" One of the many explanations for this practice is that even in this moment of intense joy, we must remember that the world is still broken and it is our duty to work to fix it.

Weddings, as other celebratory Jewish occasions, are marked with a festive meal, seudat mitvah, shared with family and friends. Joyous dancing is often a part of this celebration.

Using this Book at Home

Consider using the detailed illustrations of this book to seek out its uniquely Jewish aspects. Examine the drawing of the interior of the sanctuary where Minnie and Morris have come to be married. See if your children can locate the ark, the chuppah, the menorahs, the symbol of the Ten Commandments, and the Jewish stars. On how many pages can you and your children spot Hebrew letters?

Discuss with your children what lessons may be learned from Minnie's and Morris' choices.
- What motivated Morris to plan a fancy wedding?
- Would Minnie and Morris have had friends to share in the joy of the wedding ceremony and reception if things had been less fancy?
- At first, Minnie was quite practical in her approach to the wedding. Why did she eventually acquiesce and join Morris in his extravagant plans?
- What effect did the couple's plans have on their friends? How would you have reacted if you had been a friend of Morris and Minnie? Why didn't the couple anticipate how their actions might affect others?
- Why did the newlyweds' friends wait for them at their new flat?
- How might the couple have acted differently, and what outcomes would different choices have brought?
- What important life lessons do you think Minnie and Morris learned from their wedding experiences?

Use this story to segue to personal stories of family weddings, perhaps including humorous anecdotes. Children are often captivated by tales of such events and can gain insight into personalities and family relationships.

The Market Wedding

Cary Fagan • Art by Regolo Ricci

Adapted from a story by Abraham Cahan

TUNDRA BOOKS

Published in Canada by Tundra Books,
75 Sherbourne Street, Toronto, Ontario, M5A 2P9

Published in the United States by Tundra Books of Northern New York,
P.O. Box 1030, Plattsburgh, New York 12901

Library of Congress Catalog Number: 00-131208

Library and Archives Canada Cataloguing in Publication

Fagan, Cary
    The market wedding

Adapted from: A ghetto wedding / by Abraham Cahan.
ISBN 0-88776-492-4

I. Ricci, Regolo. II. Cahan, Abraham, 1860-1951. Ghetto wedding. III. Title.

PS8561.A375M37 2000   jC813'.54   C00-930414-2
PZ7.F33Ma 2000

The Market Wedding is adapted from the story "A Ghetto Wedding" by Abraham Cahan,
published in 1898.

We acknowledge the support of the Canada Council for the Arts
and the Ontario Arts Council for our publishing program.

We acknowledge the financial support of the Government of Canada through
the Book Publishing Industry Development Program for our publishing activities.

Design by Terri-Anne Fong

Printed and bound in China

1 2 3 4 5 6   13 12 11 10 09 08

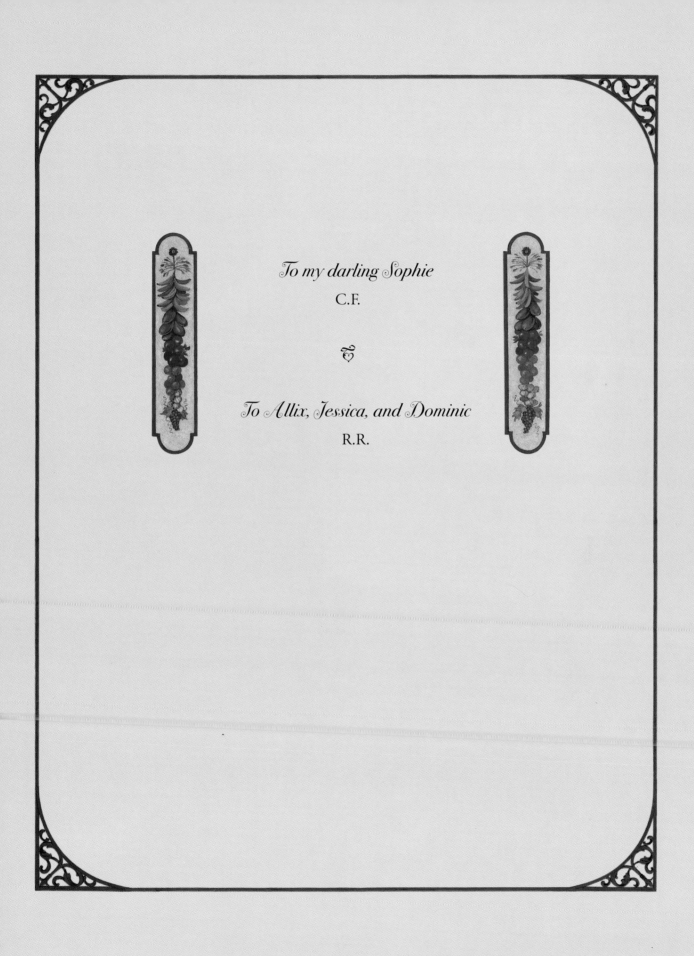

To my darling Sophie
C.F.

&

To Allix, Jessica, and Dominic
R.R.

Morris owned a fish stall in Kensington Market. All day long he shouted, "Fish for sale! Right out of the lake! Carp, sturgeon, perch, trout, walleye, flounder! Fresh fish!" His hands smelled of fish, and every night he scrubbed them with a rough soap.

Across the street, Minnie sold hats from a cart. All day long she shouted, "Hats for sale! The latest fashions, straight from Paris! Cloche hats, turbans, toques, berets, and boaters! Beautiful hats!"

One day Morris and Minnie got mixed up. "Fresh hats!" Morris cried. "Right out of the lake." Minnie called out, "The latest fish! Straight from Paris!"

They looked at each other across the street and laughed. And that was when they fell in love.

One Sunday they went to the picture show. "Minnie," whispered Morris in the dark, "I'm crazy about you. But we can't get married."

"Why not?" asked Minnie.

"Because you deserve to live like a movie star, like Mary Pickford! You should sit in the finest chair, eat from the most delicate china plates, sleep in the softest bed. And how can I give you the best just from selling fish?"

"I'm no movie star," said Minnie. "And you're no Rudolph Valentino either. Besides, I do well enough selling hats. A nice little wedding with our friends is good enough for me."

"Absolutely not," Morris insisted with a shake of his head. "It's got to be the best for my Minnie. Just you wait. Your Morris is one smart cookie. I'll think of a plan."

"A plan is just what I don't need," sighed Minnie.

*T*he next Sunday they went to the Sunnyside amusement park. On the carousel Morris said, "I've got it! I've figured out a way for us to get married."

"How?" asked Minnie.

"We'll take all the money that we've saved and make the most fancy wedding anyone has ever seen. We'll spend every last penny."

"But then we won't have any money left. Not even for furniture," Minnie said.

"We won't need any. When our friends realize what a magnificent wedding we're putting on, they will naturally feel obliged to buy us only the finest gifts. Tables, silverware, teacups, lamps, a coffee percolator – they'll give us only the best. Our home will be like a Hollywood mansion."

"You'll excuse the expression, this plan smells very fishy to me," Minnie said with a frown.

"Don't you worry," Morris said, patting her arm. "We'll soon be living in style."

Right away Morris and Minnie found a place to live for after they were married – a second-floor flat in a house on Nassau Street. The flat was empty but for two old chairs. As they looked about, Morris said, "Just wait until we have all our wedding gifts. Silk curtains. A velvet sofa. Maybe even a mirror with a gold frame."

"All right," Minnie said. "I give in. Nice things are not so hard to live with."

So they went to see Lazer the scribe. Lazer sat by his window writing letters for people to send to their relatives in the old country.

Morris told Lazer, "We want you to copy out the most beautiful wedding invitations anyone has ever seen."

"With gold ink," said Minnie.

"And a red seal," added Morris.

"Are you millionaires all of a sudden?" Lazer asked with a shrug. But he took out his best pen and began.

orris and Minnie hired a servant in red livery to deliver the invitations. But they could not resist following secretly behind to watch.

The servant made a deep bow and handed the first invitation to Leah, who ran a housewares shop.

"What's this?" Leah asked. "Is the king visiting? Is the prime minister holding a ball?"

Next was Nathan the baker. He had to wipe the flour from his hands before opening the invitation. "Gold ink!" he exclaimed with astonishment. "And a red seal! Come, Naomi," he called to his wife. "Come, children! This is something to see!" Soon all the neighbors in the market were talking at once, marveling over the invitations to Minnie and Morris's wedding.

Over the next few days, rumors about the wedding arrangements spread like wildfire. Nathan heard that Morris had rented a great hall and had hired the most expensive caterer in town. Leah said that the most renowned seamstresses were making Minnie's wedding dress. And Jacob the fruit-seller, who liked to play his violin at ordinary weddings, announced that the couple had hired the famous Casa Loma Orchestra to play the latest dance music.

*T*he day of the wedding arrived. Minnie put on her elaborate wedding gown and Morris, his shiny tuxedo. With their last few dollars they had hired a white automobile, driven by the servant in red livery, who drove them to the synagogue on Henry Street.

"I have an ache in my stomach," Minnie said nervously as they rode along. "Maybe we've gone too far."

"Don't worry, sweet pea. I bet the synagogue is more crowded than for the High Holidays. This is going to be a wedding that no one will ever forget."

The automobile stopped and the servant opened the door for them. But when Morris and Minnie entered the synagogue, what did they see? Not their friends. Not their neighbors from the market. Just ten men drowsing on the front bench as they waited for the evening prayers, and a wizened old couple who wandered in at the last moment. Where were all the people they had invited?

The rabbi began the ceremony. Morris and Minnie stood under the *chuppah* and repeated the sacred words. The bride circled the groom seven times. Then Morris stamped on a glass rolled in a napkin for good luck. *"Mazel tov!"* cried the drowsing men, their voices echoing in the empty synagogue.

Morris and Minnie were now husband and wife.

*T*he bride and groom rode in the automobile to the reception hall. The chandeliers glittered; the tables were decorated with roses and carnations; the waiters stood at attention. But when Minnie and Morris entered, they saw that all the chairs were empty. Not a single guest had come to the dinner.

Morris went back out to the street, but he found only the wizened old man and woman carrying a paper bag. He invited them inside. As they sat down, the Casa Loma Orchestra started to play.

The waiters brought soup, salad, three main courses, sherbet, cakes. The wizened old man and woman enjoyed each dish, but Minnie and Morris had no appetite.

What a disappointment! How could they have a celebration with no guests to share it? And what would they do without the gifts they had expected? They would have no table, no silverware, no rugs, no lamps. They would not even have a bed to sleep in.

"I miss our friends," Minnie said.

"Some smart cookie I am," Morris said with a groan.

*T*he wedding feast ended. The musicians packed away their instruments and the waiters cleared the tables. The wizened old man and woman had fallen asleep in their chairs. Finally they awoke and presented the couple with the paper bag. In it was a bottle of sweet wine, the only gift.

Because Minnie and Morris had used up all their money, they had to walk to the flat that they had rented. The train of Minnie's gown became soiled as it dragged on the ground, while Morris's shoes lost their shine. They trudged past the market stalls, shut up for the night, and heard a streetcar rattling along College Street.

What gloom they felt . . . what sorrow and regret filled their hearts. . . .

Silently they approached their flat in the house on Nassau
Street. As they drew nearer, Minnie and Morris noticed
a cluster of dark figures standing on the sidewalk outside.
A gang of thieves? But just then they heard a friendly voice call out,
"Here come the bride and groom!"

Why, it was Leah and her husband, Ben! And Nathan the baker, with
his family. And Jacob the fruit-seller and Lazer the scribe and all their
other friends and neighbors from the market.

"But we don't understand," Minnie said. "Why didn't you all come
to the wedding?"

The group became silent and looked down. Finally Nathan the baker
spoke. "We were ashamed."

"Ashamed?" Morris said. "But why?"

"Because we did not own clothes fine enough for such a splendid
wedding. And we did not think our gifts were good enough either.
So we decided it was better not to come at all."

"What fools we've been," said Minnie. "But at least you can all
come inside and warm yourselves before going home."

So everyone followed the bride and groom into the house and up the stairs. They all crowded into the flat. Without even a lamp, they had to see by the moonlight coming in through the window.

"We could make a toast," Morris said, remembering the bottle of sweet wine. "But we don't even have glasses."

"I can bring some from my shop," said Leah. She hurried to get them and, when she came back, Morris poured everyone a drink.

"Maybe people are hungry," Nathan said. "I just baked some rye buns." And out he ran.

"And I'll bring oranges," Jacob the fruit-seller added, following the baker.

When they returned, everyone raised their glasses. *"L'chaim!"* they cried. "A long and happy life for the bride and groom!"

*J*acob had also brought his violin. "If no one objects, perhaps I could play a little music," he said shyly.

"Play! Play!" Minnie and Morris said together.

So music filled the flat, the brisk melody of the *hora*. The friends joined hands and danced in a circle. They coaxed Morris and Minnie to sit in the two old chairs, and lifted them into the air, parading the newlyweds about.

What laughing! What talking! What eating and dancing!

*T*he dancing went on for hours. As the guests grew tired, they realized that there was nowhere to sit down but the two old chairs. In fact, the flat was bare! Someone ran home to get an old lamp, another a rug, a third some pots to cook in. Before long, the flat was almost furnished.

"We've brought everything but a bed," Nathan the baker said. "Nobody has one to spare."

"We do," came two wizened old voices. They all turned to see the old man and old woman, the only guests from the synagogue. "Our children used to sleep in it," the old woman said, "but now they are grown up. We just live nearby, but we don't have the strength to carry it ourselves."

"Bring it up, bring it up!" everyone cried. They jostled one another in their eagerness to help. The bed was rather old-fashioned, but it fit the bedroom perfectly.

"Thank you," said Morris and Minnie, and they blushed.

At last the guests went home. Minnie and Morris put on their nightshirts and went to bed. In the moonlight they could see all the gifts. Nothing was new or fancy or fit for a movie star, but all of it was precious to them.

The very next day they were back at work in the market.

"Buy a fish and get a free hat!" Morris cried.

"Buy a hat and get a free fish!" Minnie called.

And so they lived and were happy.